ABSINTHE : A Journal of World Literature in Translation is published twice a year by the Department of Comparative Literature at the University of Michigan.

ABSINTHE : A Journal of World Literature in Translation receives the generous support of the following schools, offices and programs at the University of Michigan: Rackham Graduate School, Office of the Vice Provost for Global and Engaged Education, Institute for the Humanities, International Institute, Armenian Studies Program, and the Kenneth G. Lieberthal and Richard H. Rogel Center for Chinese Studies.

Correspondence should be addressed to

ABSINTHE : A Journal of World Literature in Translation
Department of Comparative Literature
2015 Tisch Hall
435 South State Street
Ann Arbor, MI 48109-1003

Typesetting and Design
William Kalvin, Delmas Typesetting. Ann Arbor, Michigan
delmastype.com

ISBN : 978-1-60785-509-5
ISSN : 1543-8449

sites.lsa.umich.edu/absinthe
Follow us on Twitter : @AbsintheJournal

ABSINTHE : *A Journal of World Literature in Translation*

DWAYNE HAYES	FOUNDING EDITOR
SILKE-MARIA WEINECK	EDITOR-IN-CHIEF
YOPIE PRINS	CHAIR OF COMPARATIVE LITERATURE *at* THE UNIVERSITY OF MICHIGAN—PUBLISHER
JUDITH GRAY	ADMINISTRATOR
MEGAN BERKOBIEN, ELISABETH FERTIG, GRAHAM LIDDELL, *and* GENTA NISHKU	MANAGING EDITORS
ALI BOLCAKAN, WILL STROEBEL, *and* PETER VORISSIS	EDITORS

ABSINTHE

WORLD LITERATURE IN TRANSLATION

WORLD HELLENISMS

ABSINTHE 24 | FALL 2018

ABSINTHE 24   TABLE OF CONTENTS

FROM THE EDITORS

Why "World Hellenisms"? What were we thinking when we sent this issue to press with such a name? The phrase seems to invite disaster on multiple fronts.

First, there's the opacity of "Hellenisms." Why the plural? What precisely do these Hellenisms mean? Then, of course, there's the breadth of its scope—"World"—one whose weight our issue can hardly hope to bear in any real sense. Nor indeed would we want to. There are very real political problems lurking within any encyclopedic claim to represent the whole world over. And yet, here we are with the word "world" in our title. At the risk of making empty promises to our readers, promises that this issue will lead them, like Lucian's *True Story*, across vast, fantastical geographies, over seas of milk or, indeed, through the outer arc of space itself, where they might contemplate our planet as some seamless, unified entity, we've chosen the word "world" with quite a different aim in mind: to push (and prod) Hellenism beyond its geographic and cultural comfort zones, to set it tumbling off beyond the borders (and we mean both external and internal borders) of its stifling nation-state, in a wide-ranging but always site-specific and localized itinerary. At each stop along the way, we wanted this Greekness to find its plurals—hence the "Hellenisms" of our title. While they present no unified topography, tongue or even topic, these Hellenisms map out the contours of a shared conversation.

Surely today's Hellenism isn't limited to Hellas, nor to the Hellenic language. We looked for writings that explored Greece from the perspective of visitors, displaced persons, and marginalized people looking in, or, conversely, from the perspective of locals striving to break out. We looked for non-Greek texts set in non-Greek locales that traced the Hellenisms of their own place and history. We looked for representations of Greekness that productively unsettled us with their unfamiliarity.

Rather than attempting to settle on a singular definition, however broad, we hope that the selection of texts in this issue suggests a shifting, prismatic quality to the notion of the "Hellenic." Speaking from multiple languages, through multiple translators, and across multiple forms—fiction and non-fiction, prose and poetry—the texts that we've assembled here create a kind of din, like a motley group of travelers pausing at an inn for the night before they continue on their way(s) the next day. Listen closely, however, and you'll hear them interacting, debating, laughing at shared jokes or mourning lost friends. They engage creatively with the archetypes of Greek mythology (Boukova, Hooleh), reflect on the history and politics of the Greece of today and of a century ago, through the streets of Athens and across the Aegean (Chouliaras, Shoshkes, Capossela), and even delve into the well-trod libraries of the Modern Greek literary canon (Sotiropoulos, Emam, both tracking the liminal figure of Cavafy in France and Egypt, respectively). We were inspired by the idea of travel more generally, of movement across time and space, beginning with the stifling enclosure of Kastrisiou's haunting story, following Polygeni's lyrical orbits and explorations, and ending with Ioannou's questioning of the future.

Only by traveling alongside them will you understand what these Hellenisms mean.

We also would like to thank the *Absinthe* team, Megan Berkobien, Elisabeth Fertig, Graham Liddell and Genta Nishku, for their invaluable contributions towards putting this issue together.

The editors would like to extend special thanks to Professor Vassilios Lambropoulos and Professor Artemis Leontis from the Modern Greek Studies Program at the University of Michigan, and to Dr. Etienne Charrière for their help with this issue.

This publication is made possible by the generous support of the Modern Greek Studies program and the Constantine Tsangadas Trust.

Ali Bolcakan
Will Stroebel
Peter Vorissis
The University of Michigan

MATA KASTRISIOU

"Milk out of Snow"

(fiction)

Translated from the Modern Greek by Jane Assimakopoulos

We live amidst still waters. Mother calls it a lake, I don't know what to tell you. I only stare out the window and the picture is always the same. In winter when the lake freezes over, I venture out of the house and walk on the smooth surface. I take a few halting steps and then fall—clumsy person that I am—on the crystal-like surface that reflects my unfamiliar (to me) image. My life is projected through a dirty square windowpane. Mother doesn't let me go even as far as the storeroom to find a dust-cloth to clean it. She keeps me tied in the wooden chair in front of the window so I won't miss out, even for a moment, on the beautiful view. Why, just the other night I told her, "Mother, don't be afraid, take your teeth out of my hand, I'm not going anywhere. Take your teeth out of me and I'll still love you." Then she released my hand and began furiously biting her own, while screaming to me, "Well is this what you want? Is this what you want?" And so I again reached my hand out toward her with a slow almost ritual motion and suddenly I felt my love for her growing.

I can't remember how many times I've seen the lake thaw and freeze again, though I shouldn't be so ungrateful. Mother celebrates my birthday every year by making me a large cake, most often out of moldy marmalade. It doesn't taste all that bad, and even if it did, it would upset me terribly if I had to be separated for a few hours from Mother just so she could go into town to shop. This year I received an unexpected gift for my birthday. Before the sun had even come up she came to my bed and undid the bandages that have for years now been tightly wrapped around my chest. Then she kissed me tenderly on the forehead and went out of the room, leaving me all alone with this new feeling. Mother is affectionate toward me and I know that my whole life I owe to her. I said I don't remember exactly how old I am, but I feel like an infant just a few months old, a baby groping with its hands, its eyes and its voracious mouth for its mother's nipple to lull it to sleep.

The truth is that our few remaining relatives don't understand the amount of care Mother gives me. They accuse her of keeping me shut away in here, but tell me, really, don't they see that outside the window is an endless expanse of frozen lakes? Where could I possibly go in such bitter cold? Mother wants nothing to do with them, and I sense in them a threat, a threat that could all too easily disturb the calm and the order in our life. A few weeks ago a distant nephew of Mother's paid us a visit, and he hadn't even finished drinking his tea when he began spouting theories about how wrong it was to keep me so isolated. Mother was unfazed as always, but I couldn't take it and I lost control. I pounced on him and scratched his face with my fingernails until it bled. He rushed out the door of our house and went off howling. I watched him from the window running like a madman over the frozen lake, slipping, falling, and propping himself on his palms to get up, with his palms sticking to the ice leaving tiny specks of blood punishing the crystal surface.

As I understand it from what Mother has told me we live in a city filled with bridges. Small boats come and go on the lakes and all the legends of our people have to do with water. Mother will not tell me the name of the city, she's afraid that one day while she's asleep I will open the door and leave. How silly of her not to know that I would never do that because I know very well how protected I am in here. Beyond the lake lies a vast world, unfamiliar and dangerous. Here, I only hear the quiet of the snow, and of course I watch. Through the windowpane I see snowflakes falling on the sole tree that has not yet been scorched by the storm. At this time of year night never falls on the lake. Even at midnight the sky never darkens, there is just a dim light spreading out, that fleeting pale blue afternoon hue that at other times lasts just a minute, a mere minute before the sun sets. For years I have counted up these seconds before the day disappears behind the mountains, I keep them in my mind, and I imagine that those seconds are the exact time it takes for the soul to leave the body, and that they differ according to how hot or cold it is, according to the position of the moon above the earth. But now the sun is continuously at half-mast, and motionless. Pinned in place. So I could say that there are times I forget when the days or the months change, the water-color of the sky never ends, the snow merely dilutes it, fades it, and makes it less concentrated.

When I was young I too used to draw on square-shaped paper but my drawings were always so empty. The whole page white and in the middle a tree or a small killed animal. I once tried to run away, to go as far as I could from the house to see what was behind the glass pane and then to draw it on the surface of my paper, so as not to see it empty. I came back two days later. Mother was holding a large pair of scissors in her hand and her gaze was cold and she was waiting for me. She pinched my cheek so hard that tiny red stars broke out on my skin. With one swift motion she cut off my hair, she hoisted me up on the kitchen table and lifted my dress up high. She opened my legs and with a furious look in her eyes she said, "Oh no, don't tell me . . ." and then she sat me down to eat my dinner, we had instant broth and it was the first time I didn't like the food she had made for me. But I really loved my hair. And I wanted it long. So I mustn't ever leave again. And I loved my mother very much. And I wanted her near me. And so I stayed.

From that moment on we have slept in the same room. Our beds side by side. I hear her snoring, coughing and choking in her sleep and I wonder how close someone must be to you to let you live amidst her sighs and her nightmares. I watch her sleep and I see her growing older in her sleep. I remain the same. Like the landscape outside our window. The seasons pass over me and leave no trace. Only the tiny broken stars grow larger with time, grow older, and my face becomes a bloodied canvas. One night I hoisted up my dress exactly the way mother had done and muttered to myself, "Oh no, don't tell me . . ." and then I disappeared inside a pool of red water-paint in a way that might make someone say, "How silly of her . . . She was born next to a vast watery surface and look at her now, drowning in a few drops of color." I got up from my chair and went to the kitchen. In my windowpane, there I was, a small, bloodied animal on a white sheet of paper.

I killed Mother only last night. I didn't intend to do it. She woke up from our sleep with a start and began breathing with difficulty. "Bring some water," she howled. "Why are you looking at me like a milkfish?" And I took the pillow from my bed and I put it over her face. Nearer to me than ever, closer to me than ever before, I felt her beneath my hands, struggling, sweating and perhaps crying. When her chest stopped heaving, I got up shaking and left the house. With the large poker we use to turn logs in the fireplace I tried for hours to break through the ice, until finally I managed it just before dawn. I was hurting and suffering from the cold but that didn't frighten me as much as the fact that the whole time I was smashing the ice, I seemed to also be smashing the reflection of my sickly eyes on the ice. My pale, tightly drawn lips and severe cheekbones. I went back home and paced all around the house. I opened Mother's trunk and found a diary hidden there and a large book with the legends of my country. The date showed it was Christmas Eve. Not being so good with dates, I know that this holiday, for me, is nothing but another day with dim pale blue light. I lifted my mother from the bed and took her in my arms. She was light and still warm. I went outside and began walking on the frozen marble. When I reached the hole

I knelt and looked at my mother for a moment, but I didn't recognize her. Perhaps that was my punishment. I let her slide down into the water and watched her disappear with the white of her nightgown up over her shoulders. Oh no, don't tell me . . .

In the center of my city today they will be celebrating Christmas. Legend has it that the eldest female child of the household, dressed in a white tunic, goes round the houses door-to-door humming an old Neapolitan tune. I don't know where Naples is, but the photograph in the book shows beautiful girls there, with ample bust-lines and quite alluring eyes. But I don't know if they have mothers, too. One can't have everything. In a little while I will get up from my chair and go outside. At the spot where I made the hole, the water will have frozen over again and I won't know where my mother is buried. She may even still be sleeping in the bed next to mine. I'm not really sure. I should have marked the spot. But how? There's nothing but a white sheet of paper with a tree, and a killed animal in the center. I read in the book that in the depths of the lake is the city of the dead. Nonsense. If the dead live down there, who are we, living up here?

YIORGOS CHOULIARAS

"Refugees"

(poetry)

Translated from the Modern Greek by David Mason
& the author

Refugees

On the other side
of the photograph I write to remind myself
not where and when but who
I am not in the photograph
They left us nothing
to take with us
Only this photograph
If you turn it over you will see me
Is that you in the photograph, they ask me
I don't know what to tell you

CHAIM SHOSHKES

"Old-New Greece"

(non-fiction)

Translated from the Yiddish by William Gertz Runyan

Athens, the capital of Greece, even possesses an underground railway line, and over three hundred thousand inhabitants, most with crooked noses and eyes as if glossed with oil. Athens is inundated with sun and also with dust, despite the gleaming asphalt of its streets. But who looks at this setting in the first moments after arrival? All eyes are drawn to the great mountain, to the Acropolis where 2,400 years ago monumental temples were raised to the almighty gods, gathering places and theaters arranged for the demos, grandstands for the Greek sages and rulers, and for the rebellious—prisons.

Under the burning southern sun we climb up to the ancient temples of Zeus, the almighty "god in chief," to the separate temple of his heavenly consort, the goddess Zika.

We enter the stone amphitheater, where five thousand ancient Greeks used to admire the marvelous tragedies of their inspired dramatists.

And here to the side stands the temple of Vesta, where the gods were served intimately indeed. Just as, for example, in a covert love parlor forbidden by the law in our great cities . . .

And just cast your glance from this high mountain down to the underlying new city and its streets, which look like narrow lines, and to the streetcars that give the impression of playthings—you'll understand why the old residents of the Acropolis were so proud of themselves and their gods: on this mountain one must feel far above the average cut of human.

And now at a distance you see remnants of the lockup where Socrates ended his life. And off to the side stand the ruins of the academy that bestowed Greek philosophy to the world.

Marble columns, thousands of columns in varied decorative styles, massive with the finest nuances of color, give testament to the great, proud people that lived on this mountain; this was a mighty democracy that heard Demosthenes speak, bent beneath the biting satire of Diogenes, placed its trust in the lawgivers Dracon and Solon—but a democracy that was later broken by the mighty fist of barbarian rulers.

An intermixing of peoples occurred here, tens of races and lineages crossed here and created a new Levantine type.

The ancient columns remained, but the ancient Greeks cannot at all recognize the inhabitants of today's Greece as the descendants of the classically molded Athens of old. You need only observe the city below, the facial features so distant from the old type that remains forever in marble, to be persuaded.

* * *

The sun, the climate breed indolence, and although it's midday the coffee houses are full of people spiritedly conversing and gesticulating no less adeptly than our Jews. Nothing more, everything here costs half, they sit and chat because there's nothing else to do. They broker and deal, hatch harebrained schemes and mostly talk politics.

How do I know this if I don't understand Greek, either the ancient Homeric language or the new one of the nimble merchants?

The story is that a tall graying man at a nearby table, hearing our Polish, addressed us asking whether we understood Russian. It turns out that this is the current attaché of Yugoslavia in Greece. Once he held the same position in Russia. He has little to do himself and is pleased at the opportunity to converse a bit. Here they love to do so with a cup of coffee and four glasses of cold water.

Our Yugoslavian doesn't have a high opinion of the Greek's political reliability.

"You see," he says, "the whole public, today they're ardent republicans; all of Greece has sent only twenty monarchists to parliament out of two hundred and eighty deputies, but when another breeze starts blowing, the situation will be the other way round. The former premier Pangalos, so beloved a year ago, was just released from prison—don't be surprised if a year from now Pangalos' place in prison is taken by another premier. They even say there's a special cell for the premier with every comfort . . ."

Leaving the coffee house we notice a sign in Russian and Greek: "Russian bar."

We go in. A typical big city bar with hot and cold fare, full of plates and covered in a host of flies.

At the register a fat Russian with a broad smiling face, we give a cordial greeting. He hasn't been a restaurateur his whole life either, all told he was the chief of a military court in Crimea under Wrangel, now he dishes out other orders, but it makes no difference: he's not doing too badly, thank God. There are several hundred Russians here, mostly former White officers and their families, who after the great collapse also sailed to Greek shores.

A young Russian waitress serves the table. It's enough to see her hands with their long fingers to be convinced that fate intended her for something other than working in a dirty bar serving guests who aren't overly clean.

A short chat: the daughter of a Cuban military doctor, her father died on the way from Crimea to Constantinople—the young girl wanders homeless, becomes a dancer at a cabaret, goes through hell . . .

"Oh, my friend, things are good for me now, I'm earning an honest bit of bread . . ."

Tears appear in her weary but still beautiful eyes: Exile!

The few Russian Jews who migrated here are quite well established, but distant from and ignorant of Judaism.

It's enough to mention that none of them could tell me if there was a synagogue, a rabbi or Jews at all.

The Russians at least have a communal club—but the Russian Jews convene either at the stock market or in the nightclubs.

* * *

But I found no rest until I clarified one of the facts of which *contemporary* Greece can be proud and which is very instructive, especially for us Jews. That is the question of how they accommodated the million Greeks who emigrated from Turkey and how the resettlement of a million Turks who emigrated from Greece was arranged.

A whole day I searched for someone who could explain this to me. I even went to a newspaper office to this end, but the only language understood anywhere was Greek.

Once I had already lost hope of learning anything, chance came to my aid: in the evening we were sitting in the large garden Zasion, which is outfitted with the greatest luxury and where for one of our *zloty* you can drink good beer while also taking in music and a variety show.

The garden was full and it occurred to me to ask the waiter, who understood French, if there wasn't a journalist or state official here with whom I could converse in French or German. A half hour later the waiter approached me with a gentleman whom he presented as an official from the Ministry of Justice.

This official spoke fluent French and turned out to be one of those Greeks driven out by the Turkish government.

It wasn't at all long ago, in 1923, that the Greeks wanted to take

Anatolia from the Turks, and another couple provinces to boot. At the outset this was going very well. They made it all the way to Constantinople. Then their luck turned and Kemal Pasha broke the Greek army, drove it out deep into the land and later said: "You want our Anatolia because more than a million Greeks live there; but I'll make it otherwise: I'll leave Anatolia for Turkey and you can take back your million Greeks—eat them in good health and bon appétit."

"And perhaps you'd like the Greeks of Constantinople, from Angora—here, take them back and may it do you good." In other words, he "pulled a Turk" as they say, began to drive the Turkish Greeks to their old fatherland.

So what does Greece do? She also has around a million Turks and Macedonians, she answered with the same sentiment and began driving them to Turkey.

All this transpired in recent years—we all read about it in the papers. But none of us had any concept of the awful calamity that erupted here.

Moving *two million* people from one place to another—that is something that occurs seldom in history.

But this effort did not turn out badly. A Greek Resettlement Commission was created, as was an American aid committee.

And the homes of the Turks in Macedonia were settled and aid was received by the Greeks who poured in, the Turks did the same in Anatolia.

With the help of America and an internal loan, the government provided land and implements with which to work it.

For the urban population, small but comfortable houses were built in various areas.

I saw this new city, which extends for several kilometers from Port Piraeus to Athens and, all told, is populated by around a hundred thousand formerly homeless Greeks.

The resettlement has gone on for six years already—it hasn't ended yet, but in ancient Greece too they built temples for the gods of Olympus and in that brought humanity pride. Contemporary Greeks may take pride in the great humanitarian work of sympathy and brotherly love that will remain forever in history.

❋ ❋ ❋

18

Late at night a small ship carried us from Paleron harbor to the ship *President Wilson*, where we reside.

The moon lit the enchanted mountain of the Acropolis, where the pagan temples were brilliantly crafted.

So many gods, so many cults—cold marble without soul, without life.

We Jews haven't left the world even one column. We don't possess even one temple more than two thousand years old—but did bestow an *amud haesh*, a column of fire to humanity . . .

Don't ask me why I parted so coldly with the land of the Olympians . . .

MARYAM HOOLEH

"Athena"

(poetry)

Translated from the Persian by Cameron Cross

Athena

See, how down we tumbled
And the spectacle through and through
    Licked our faith
We kept clear of the dogs
Until our heart
Hung from the howls of civilization
All expansive hopes
With the groan of narcissism
Sank
    Into the graveyard of human limbs
And nothing but shoes
    Remained . . .
See, how the Kurds have brought
Vagrancy
To Athens' portico
And the whores of Albania
Walk
    On torn and tattered veils
    And the tiled floor of the dead
And drape the mottled arms of beauty-spots
    Over last century's cabarets
And set the lock
What a strange dance!
As birds
With severed necks
    Fly
    Over the PKK's wall
And as patriots
With broken teeth
    Spit
And hatred and helplessness
Form a brotherhood
Ah —
    How I adore painting
    Yet at the same time
    I loathe

Every kind of shirt
As for the painters
In democracy's capital —
        Behead them
Only their fingernails have been capable
Of planting a flag in my heart
Flag
Flag
All this color
Is no longer worth nature's glory
The rainbow hangs from the gibbet
And no color
Has refuge
In the arms of another
Flaunting the residence permit
Showers from its dawn
        With the kernel of hope
Until the clouds
In an astonishing assembly
        Form
The image of calcified prophets
And dream men
All become believers
Don't ask that one to take my hand
Don't ask that one
To gather my feet
        From the surface of the mire
That one obeys their shoe
(And the shoe will forever
Madly
        Traverse
The blisters and blood
With an armload of firewood and beer)
Until breaking
See, how down we tumbled
And my heart poured out
From the hair of youth
As one estranged

My mother guesses you
And you join in
Her weeping over me
O Freedom
No one knew
How they had
         To embrace you
Next winter
I'll worship
The forests of your song
In the fireplace
Next spring
Zarathustra's children
Will kill him
Like the new-year bonfire
And I know nothing
About you
In one hand heroin
And silver in the other
I'll go to the Omonoia Square
And lay out my wares
And tomorrow
I'll invite you
To a game of billiards
And order a debate
For you
Not knowing that last night
In a road of darkness
Tehran
Has killed you
And that in the morning
The BBC
Has licked
Your wounds
With measured ruminations
If I lost
Convince me
To forever wear black

And light two candles
Upon my shoes

     Athens, August 23, 1998

ERSI SOTIROPOULOS

From *What's Left of the Night* (New Vessel Press)

(fiction)

Translated from the Modern Greek by Karen Emmerich

Eyes closed, I turned toward you in bed. I stretched a hand through the half-light to touch your shoulder. That exquisite curve, the pale skin, paler against the dirty sheet. Nothing written on skin can be erased, I told myself. Five years ago, at a similar hour, you stirred in your sleep and your thigh brushed against me. I was still wearing my shirt. My hand slid over your chest, which was hairless and tawny with an undertone of ochre. I remember it strong, hairless, bright. The line of your mouth, that pink, open circle, and the gleam of a tooth, barely visible. A bit of dried saliva. I traced your lips with my fingers. Then my hand crept lower, lower still. You breathed, snoring slightly. In your sleep you rolled over and wrapped your arms around me. You murmured a word I didn't know. Perhaps you were thirsty. My hand opened and closed . . .

A shudder swept over the empty bed. I'd left the window open and the curtains fluttered in the Parisian breeze. It was time I abandoned these rêveries. John would be waiting in the lobby.

The earth still seemed flat then, and night fell all at once until the end of the world, where someone hunched in the light of a lamp would be able to see, centuries later, a red sun setting over ruins, would be able to see, beyond seas and ruined harbors, countries lost in time living in the glow of triumph, in the slow agony of defeat. History repeats itself, he thought, though he wasn't sure whether it really was repetition. His talent and persistence alone would allow him to see. Gripping his pen, he listened. Sounds, lights, smells, it all came flooding back. It was night once more on the flat earth. Voices reached his ears. A strain of cheap music from Attarin where the shops were open late, the sound of a barrel organ whose saccharine melody swelled and overflowed and climbed the muddy stairs. In the rooms upstairs limbs mingled on threadbare sheets. For half an hour of perfect pleasure, half an hour of absolute, sensual pleasure. Limbs, lips, eyelids on the squalid bed, kisses, gasping mouths. Then they would leave separately like fugitives, knowing this half an hour would haunt the rest of their lives, knowing they would return to seek it again. But now all they wanted was for the night to swallow them up, and as each hurried down the stairs that unbearable tinkle of music greeted him once more, a wobbly chime that mocked the oppressive thud of his heart. The street outside was always deserted, and the foot-steps of an invisible shadow would echo in the distance, then fade. He'd stand for a moment in the doorway, then button his coat and walk quickly away, hugging the wall, head bent, collar raised. And sometimes it happened, it had in fact happened, that his eyes would meet the eyes of another man skidding like a rat through the darkness, some nervous, well-dressed man coming from the other direction, heading hypnotized toward those same stairs, that same room, to roll over those same stained sheets.

And if the lovers don't respond to your touch? he thought. If they're warm, soft-skinned statues that receive all caresses with the indifference of works of art? That Platonic idea enticed him, but only to a point. The object of desire was so distant, so close. Lips, limbs, bodies. Lips, gasping mouths. That was what he should write about. So close, so distant. That was the purpose of art, to abolish distance.

He recalled the figure of a youth from years ago. Had it been in Constantinople? Yeniköy? A beardless youth working as an ironmonger's apprentice, and as the boy bent half naked over the anvil, sparks flying onto his glistening chest, he saw his face lit heroically, imagined him crowned with vines and bay leaves. They hadn't spoken, and he never saw him again. Who would write about him? Who would heave him up out of the oblivion of History?

Years later, someone hunched in the light of a lamp would be able to see a red sun setting over mythical cities, would see burning grass through rusted iron, where once a marble fountain spurted water and the last droplets ran dry in the evening light. He would see the crimson rays shining on the young body of the apprentice in Yeniköy, fleetingly illuminating a possibility, yes, a possibility that assumed substance, an almost material substance, as that same youth now weaved between the columns of an ancient agora among the crowds of Antioch or Seleucia, and many were they who praised his beauty.

That "years later" is now, he thought. He alone could see. Only he wasn't yet ready. His impatience chafed at him, and contrived miserable, graceless poems, which he tore up in self-reproach. And then there was that clunky pastiche . . . A heap of adjectives and too-fine turns of phrase, the churning runoff of a lyricism he hated but didn't know how to leave behind. How can I shake free of that sentimental burden? he wondered. Often during the day he felt useless, irresolute, a failure. The problem was Alexandria, the city stifled him. His provincial life, his circle of silly people with their unshakable self-confidence, the feluccas and *fellahin*, the landscape like a cobwebbed stencil whose heavy humidity sank into your bones—it all weakened his nerves. And often

30

he determined, without really believing it, that he needed to erase the Alexandria within him if he really wanted to write.

But now he was in a foreign city that charmed and repelled him in equal measure, a cosmopolitan capital that glittered with refinement, whose smallest corner seemed large and important. He needed to resist his bad mood and find a way to enjoy these final few days of the trip. No more wavering, he thought, I'll make a daily schedule and stick to it. He reflexively straightened his tie and descended the three steps into the hotel lobby.

"Monsieur Cavafy!" he heard someone call.

The large hall was empty, its central chandelier lit above a marble floor that shone like the surface of a lake. The aged concierge was moving slowly in his direction.

"Monsieur Cavafy, your brother was waiting for you. He left just a few moments ago for Café de la Paix."

It was a warm summer evening, the temperature around eighty degrees Fahrenheit. Mild weather with a salutary wind. Perfect for the light redingote he was wearing. A good thing he hadn't decided on his heavy linen jacket, he thought, a good thing indeed, and quickened his pace. But as he walked swiftly, following the flow along the boulevard, where coachmen trundled toward the Opéra brandishing their whips, he felt the moroseness that plagued him coming back and knew that sooner or later the familiar unease would descend upon him again.

"Costis, I finished it," John called as soon as he caught sight of him.

He appeared to be in a magnificent mood. He was holding the manuscript in his hand and waving it in the air like a trophy.

The waiter set two steaming cups of chocolate on the table.

"Thank you for thinking of me," he said, though he would have preferred a cold tea.

"Well?" John asked with a wide smile.

"I'm late. I must have fallen asleep."

"I'm sure it's done you good."

He noticed an old woman coming toward them, hand outstretched, dragging one leg. Her hair was matted and every so often she stumbled.

"Give her something. I can't bear to look at her."

The old woman came over to their table, casting a gluttonous glance at the plate of petit fours.

"Give her something," he said again. He glanced at the manuscript, now rolled into a tube in his brother's hand. He could make out a few letters, slightly slanted with the tails of the *p*'s and the *y*'s curving elaborately upward.

John stood and dropped a few coins into the woman's hand.

"*Dieu vous bénisse,*" she said. Some of her teeth were missing.

"*Dieu* doesn't seem to have blessed you, poor thing."

She dragged herself like a bundle of rags to the neighboring table and stretched out her hand beseechingly.

"But why?" John wondered. "Why should we accept squalor when it's depicted in a painting, even praise its aesthetic value? Whereas in real life we reject it. That woman could be beautiful. Everything can be beautiful. It depends on one's point of view—or, to be more precise, on the mental disposition of the viewer—"

"We can't call just anything beautiful," he said, cutting his brother off.

"Of course, anything that makes us feel, why not?"

"Even an animal? That old woman has the beauty of a sow in mud."

"There isn't just one kind of beauty," John began, then fell silent. As always when he tried to find the precise words to express an idea, he got tangled up in his own train of thought. He sipped his chocolate, then stirred it slowly with the little spoon. "Why must you be so absolute," he said, as if it weren't a question. "Sometimes I wonder . . . It's quite unfair, in the last analysis." He wasn't looking at him, as if he might be addressing some random passerby in the street, or all of Paris.

"Let me read it," he said, and reached out a hand to take the manuscript.

This was their free afternoon. They had agreed over lunch at Le Procope to take this chance to rest and reflect, to recall certain moments from the month and a half they'd been traveling, to dust off forgotten details. They both enjoyed comparing their accounts of things and they did so often, savoring that moment when the simplest incident took on a strange quality, an almost unexpected turn as the words to describe it were shaped and rounded in the other's mouth. At this point there was a whole host of events for them to remember and laugh over, getting a foretaste of the responses their stories would evoke when they were back in Alexandria, laughing at the fiascoes of their trip, like their aunt's flatulence at dinner in Holland Park, not one, not two, but three superb, resounding farts in quick succession; the others at the table had coughed to cover the sound, but even that didn't solve the problem since an unbearable stench began to spread, and one by one they rose from the table as their aunt in her black, collared pelerine kept protesting, But where are you going, my dears, I hope the perch hasn't upset you, it must have been the perch—and ever since, whenever anything odd or untoward happened, they would say to each other, "It must have been the perch."

Mother will love the story about the fart, she'll make us tell it over and over, he thought. It must have been the perch, he repeated inwardly and almost laughed aloud. Out the corner of his eye he saw John watching him and waiting.

"I like it," he said and gave a dry cough. "It's a very solid poem. I'd like to read it again."

His tone of voice struck him as false. And why the devil had he coughed? They were always perfectly frank with each other, or at least so he believed, only today he had a feeling he should watch his words. It was no small thing, what he'd let slip yesterday. In the middle of dinner as they bent over their crispy squab with peas, chatting lightly about some literary subject that he could no longer remember, he'd mentioned *en passant*: "There isn't room for two poets in one family." He'd regretted it immediately. At first John pretended not to hear, didn't respond. But a few moments later he raised his glass, saying: "In that case I suppose I'll have to make way. Cheers . . . *à ta santé!*"

His efforts to mend the breach kept them talking late into the night, and he'd been the one to suggest that his brother rewrite an old poem and change its setting to the fire at the Bazar de la Charité, from which Paris was still reeling. The occasion for the earlier version had been a snippet of conversation a friend of John's overheard at an art opening in Alexandria. A Greek society lady, the wife of a successful merchant— the friend hadn't given her name—was gazing at a painting of a setting sun smeared with purples and reds, and leaned on the shoulder of the man beside her, a well-known figure in the Greek community, likewise married—the friend hadn't given his name, either—and whispered with a heavy sigh: "I'd prefer to set in your arms." He had found it insipid, the metaphor or allegory, whatever it was, but John laughed and jotted it down. He later wrote a poem about the bombing of Alexandria in 1882 and the conflagration that followed. In the poem, the genteel lady's words served as an ironic counterpoint to the catastrophe and the vandalism that subsequently swept the city. The composition was weak and unnecessarily overblown, he'd observed to his brother. The phrase in question was absent from the present version of the poem, but an equally distasteful "sunset of friendship and feelings" had crept in. Just listen to that, sunset of friendship and feelings!

"Did you notice the second stanza?" John asked. "I'll read it to you in Greek, I translated it and the rhyme works better." He twirled his mustache before beginning the recitation:

Charred are the corsets and crinolines
ashes the silken sash,
burned are the skirts of which to now
lavender freshened the stash.

"I wanted," he continued, "to emphasize the fact that the fire at the Bazar concerns only the aristocracy. What does it matter that a few dozen servant women died in the fire? The Countess Mimmerel burned, and the Marquise of Isle. The empress's sister burned, too. That's what counts. A whole village in Brittany could have burned and there wouldn't be the same outpouring of national mourning. Do you see?"

"I agree, though I don't quite see the difference. Drama is drama."

"That doesn't mean, of course, that I was trying to write a social poem."

A failed poem, he thought. He remembered the first few days after they arrived in Paris from Marseille, when the region still smelled of sulfur and all the hotels were passing out damp towels to the ladies. And in fact the Bazar continued to burn for days, all the lace and fine linen piled inside crackling in a slow death. It had become the most popular tourist site in Paris, people came in from all the *faubourgs* to gape at the charred carcass.

"It was May 4, am I right?"

"I think so. We heard about it on the train, remember?"

At the corner of Boulevard des Capucines there was a cloud of white smoke and a crowd of coachmen, shouting. Apparently a pipe had burst. A black figure emerged from the smoke and came toward them.

"Look," he said. "Your ethereal Aphrodite is headed our way again, looking even less steady than before."

John turned to see. The beggar woman walked past on the sidewalk, staggering and bumping against the tables. A waiter came rushing out of Café de la Paix and tried to usher her away, first shouting, then shoving.

The old woman fell in a heap into the street, rolled onto her back, and started talking to the sky.

"You degrade your art," John said, his tone polite but unyielding. He unrolled the paper with the poem on it and leaned back in his chair, pretending to read.

It must have been the perch, that's what he'd like to say to Johnny now. Their aunt's words suited him perfectly today. Only he didn't know how his brother would take it. He could be quite sensitive. Then again it might make him laugh. He was about to utter the phrase when a large head with sheep-like curls and wide-open, perfectly blue eyes appeared before him.

ELENA POLYGENI

"The Shared Fate of the Heavens and of Earthly

Bodies," "The Little Station Master," and

"A HYMN OF VICTORY"

(poetry)

Translated from the Modern Greek by Holly Taylor

The Shared Fate of the Heavens and of Earthly Bodies

We all revolve around ourselves like luminous bodies. Our central axis separates desires from necessities and still begs for peace. Our other planets are strangers to us. Swirling around their own misfortunes, their loneliness. All else is simply resplendent light. The hands of earthliness touch everything the same, some earlier, suffocating in a hideous manner. The mind receives external signals, which it recycles with zeal, transforming them, habitually, into symbols. Everything tires of living, yet fears dying. The continuous flow of water reminds us of the debt of existence, to which few exceptions are judged as unacceptable. The orbit is circular, it is not ever avoided, the return to the place of departure; and there is not the slightest exception to this rule.

The Little Station Master

My sweet darkness
of a fractured, abandoned
train
I want to ascend your carriage.
Darkness dragging through my fingertips
along with the pain and trials
that have ripped
yes, have mangled
my designs.
At the station of defeat
black coffee and a biscuit
are sufficient to mourn.
What remains
of you, my melancholy
little train
No whisper, no caress
will be given.
For you, I will
be the final,
only passenger
that will grieve.

A HYMN OF VICTORY

In all the lands and in all the countries and in all the houses and throughout the ages and all the kisses and tables and funerals and beneath the illuminations and behind curtains and under quilts and hiding behind disguises and drinking champagne and within songs and inside cars and beneath flashing advertisements and on rooftops and out on balconies and within tents and breaking into laughter and breaking into fights and breaking the law and above the people and spitting on blood lines and discovering solutions and sharing progress and scorched words and above the beds and on the lips of the lethargy and within carriages and constructing palaces and on top of carpets and in schools and in ships and clutching rackets and showing limits, hand-in-hand, triumphant singing and severed heads and in all the alleys and in all the town squares, during the day and night, among velvet, the pain is bedecked and with a new saw, inviting promises, in the fresh mud, illuminating the carcasses, with the heat and the cold, in the fresh mud, and with a new saw, treading with glory, and in all the hideouts, summoning grief, and beyond the woods and beyond sorrows and beyond winters

Always,

always

the murderers

celebrate.

TAREK EMAM

From *The Second Life of Constantine Cavafy*

(fiction)

Translated from the Arabic by Anton Shammas

13.

Suddenly, he felt the bedroom air was quickly depleting.

After Alexander had left early in the morning, he locked the door and started reading, in seclusion, afraid the author of the novel might be watching him and catching him any minute. If he surprised me now, I'd die on the spot, and wouldn't be able to finish the novel.

Cavafy decided to slide open the French window and go out to the balcony. The salty air, coming from the invisible, distant blue, seeped through him, and he was astonished to realize, without knowing why, that the small, gloomy church was still in place, and suddenly felt he was no longer at his own familiar home. He remembered a large window in the Red Cross Hospital in Athens, overlooking a row of adjacent churches, separated by stripes of green lawns, making the distant asphalt road look merely like a thin dark ribbon, which was exactly what made him feel totally lost in the capital to which he had returned as a patient this time around. As for the sea, it wasn't there during his sojourn in Athens, as if one of them had to show up for the other to disappear.

Church bells began to chime, as if the melancholic Gothic buildings were waking up from sleep, emitting scary yawns in succession, according to a collective consciousness of sorts—a bell rings, and all the other iron mouths gape in hunger, echoing the lead, intertwined and interwoven, and he finds himself in another world.

He was down the first couple of days because of that gloomy scene of eternity, and not because of his illness, or the smells of antiseptics and disinfectants engulfing the air, or the cryptic doctors whom he couldn't help but think of as being masked patients. A young Greek woman in her twenties began to visit him, a poet and an outspoken journalist, all the time vigorously throwing naïve questions at him. She told him, as if reprimanding: "You should have experimented with your demotic Greek to write a popular epic as a counterpart to the Odyssey." She wrote in Katharevousa, the purest form of Modern Greek, and she strongly believed that demotic Greek had no place in poetry. Those days, there prevailed a powerful trend in insomniac Athens, advocating the return to literary Greek, in its most elevated forms, and he suddenly felt that all he had written was no longer suitable for the young generation of Greek readers, though he had never tried in earnest to publish his poetry, and he had never thought of prospective readers. His aggressive visitor made him feel doubly lost. Greece had always been a country that thought of itself as a nation, and it owned nothing but its language, which was re-sponsible for all the reasons of decline or progress, and that in particular used to annoy him and make him feel, despite it all, a certain gratitude toward that small unknown town in the south, which wasn't interested in his solitude, inside of which he felt totally removed from the contro-versies of the Capital, where poets believed they were each defending their homeland with poems.

Concerned, he asked Periklis Anastasiadis, his old friend and the man responsible for his recognition as a poet in Greece, and for giving him one hundred pounds thirty-one years ago to make the trip to his homeland, where he showed his poems to the editors of literary journals in Athens. Anastasiadis dismissed the question: "It's the young genera-tion my dear—they start off rejecting everything but then they stop short even of rebelling against what our ancestors rebelled against. We have all done the same thing, and when we reached old age, we had nothing better to do than to reread the Odyssey."

Anastasiadis' answer somehow depressed him, and he felt personal-ly insulted. For a minute he thought the young outspoken woman had been more merciful.

Being upset with Anastasiadis made him remember the latter's ad-miration for his old poems, and how he introduced him to E. M. For-ster who, in turn, introduced his poems to T. S. Eliot, T. E. Lawrence, Arnold Toynbee and others, so his poetry became familiar in Europe without a sincere desire on his part. Moreover, Anastasiadis still keeps in his possession copies of his early poems and his suggestions and critical comments on those poems which he used to send to him. This multi-plied his sense of alienation, and he simultaneously felt that Alexander was totally missing, and the Cavafy who was totally missing in the de-lirium of his illness suspected more than once the very existence of the person named Alexander.

One desperate morning, and to avoid any new discussions of art, he found the courage to speak to the outspoken young woman about the gloomy scene that was sneaking into his room through the window. She spontaneously responded: "Maybe that's better, perhaps the light will prove another tyranny. Who knows what new things it will expose?" . . .
It took him a few seconds to realize that this particular young woman had actually recited to him from his poetry, and he became jubilant like a toddler, though when he looked at the side of her face no trace of excitement was to be found.

46

At that moment of jubilation, he decided to rewrite that poem which was being recalled in that desolate morning, like a window of hope, in honor of this young woman in rags. Thirty-five years have passed since he wrote "The Windows." When he wrote it he was still living in the family house on Shereef Street, and his mother was still alive. He was thirty-four, carrying a press card of The Telegraph newspaper, and working as a stockbroker. He maintained both jobs in an equilibrium he now didn't understand. The poem came to him through the windows of the family house on that elegant and dreary street, which he was certain at the time it wouldn't change in a hundred years. Those years he still had hope, the hope which this young woman has now, that if he opened a window he'd see whatever he wants.

Cold November air gently caressed his face, and the faint fluttering of his hair made him feel calm and unruffled, made him feel the light numbness that lets his old body lose its stiffness, but once his body succumbed to the sensation, he lost his caution and didn't remember that his hand was still holding the batch of papers, and suddenly it unclasped, as if emptying its wrinkles, and he was hit by the horror of the papers of Alexander Singopoulos streaming toward the street.

14.

Stunned, he ran to gather the papers that had covered the street, his frail body moved by panic in abrupt jumps, collecting whatever he could grasp with his hands, quite certain that he wouldn't be able to catch every single sheet of paper.

The feeble thread that had kept the sheets together evaporated into thin air before they hit the ground, scattered and disgraced.

It's simply possible that some sheets had vanished between the horrifying moment of watching them floating in the air and his terrified run, crossing the living room then jumping down the stairs until he reached the street. (A child may have bent down and picked up a sheet, or maybe he snapped it while it was still gliding in the air like a mysterious creature; a loiterer may have decided to entertain his idle walk with reading a surprise gift capable of killing some moments.) But rescue arrived before he died of grief and fear and fatigue—a half-naked woman suddenly appeared from nowhere, her enormous breasts swinging and swaying in alarm, not bothered by the flimsy house gown stuck between her buttocks. When did she issue the order for all these other younger versions of herself to show up from nowhere? He wasn't sure. A flock of no longer feared scandal, whose nakedness wasn't bothered by daylight, no longer hoping for absolution. Everything had come to an end, years before they suddenly came out from the secret apartment, before they crossed the threshold, before they cheerfully joined each other to rescue a novel about which they knew nothing. They immediately set out to gather the sheets, scattered all over the street, and before he grasped what was happening, before he could watch the lugubrious scene, devotional and sincere as it was, young screams and fitful giggles and all—the woman approached him with the pile of sheets in her hands.

He tried to thank her, and to ask her why she did what she did, but he realized again that he had no voice, so he greeted her and her companions timidly, nodding repeatedly, as if to compensate for his voiceless tongue. They all exchanged smiles with him, with seductive gestures, and when he reached into the pocket of his robe, hoping to find some paper money, the woman, guessing what he was up to, preemptively and firmly grabbed his fumbling hand with hers: "We are neighbors, and floor you walk is our ceiling!"

An old poetess, and life was her only book. An Egyptian, a real madam, with the kind of English that's fit for quick bargains, whose words weren't all expected to be exactly correct. For whoever wanted her all was clear enough, as the words were bridge enough.

He couldn't refuse her invitation to enter her apartment, her mysterious brothel and the kingdom of her unrestrained nudity had, unknowingly, inspired him. But he was embarrassed because he had lost his voice. As soon as he entered the dimly lit apartment, he picked up a lone paper off a desk, and gestured with his hand for a pen, and wrote on it in English: "I beg your pardon, my lady, but I'm suffering from a temporary problem with my vocal cords." He wasn't sure of the Egyptian woman's ability to understand what he had written. Maybe she couldn't read and write, but she smiled understandingly, and started talking again the way Egyptians speak English: "I know . . . Don't worry. We missed you very much in months before, Mr. Cavafy!"

She was speaking warmly as if they were intimate neighbors. She knows! How come she does? Who told her? And he noticed that the girls scattered into their rooms with the same speed with which they had gathered the scattered sheets. Two men entered the place during the half hour in which he was sitting across from her kohl-laden eyes. She left him alone in both cases, and whisked the two men aside, talking to them in whispers that couldn't conceal the bargaining, then each disappeared into a room. Here's home for everyone.

When he stood up to excuse himself, he noticed a steady look in the woman's eyes, examining his face. She saw him to the entrance, and while she was closing the door of her paradise behind him, she hissed out a conspiratorial sentence: "You need any help—don't hesitate to knock my door. Feel at home!"

VINICIO CAPOSSELA

From *Tefteri: A Settling of Scores*

(non-fiction)

Translated from the Italian by Elettra Pauletto

The word "crisis" comes from the Greek *kríno*, which means to sep-arate, sort, divide. Crisis is a concept that lends itself well to *rebetiko*—a type of music born of separation—and to Greece, from which Europe is pulling away, driven by the disdain that lies at the root of all rejection.

People often speak of Greece with language that evokes tragedy, which, as a genre, was invented there. The word "tragedy" comes from the Greek *tragudi*, or song, and at its root is *tragos*, which means goat. *Tragodia*, song of the goat. Once the cultural mother of Europe, Greece has become a scapegoat for her sins. Europa, daughter to a king of Crete, seduced by Zeus. Europa of the "wide eyes," land of the west, ever facing the setting sun.

Since ancient times, Greek creations have been permeated with a sense of universality. Taken together, this body of work tells the story of man, the *anthropos*. And it tells the story of man and destiny, of what is happening to Westerners in this moment of "crisis," of choices.

Let's travel there, a small tool in hand—a thyrsus, perhaps—and accompanied by music born of catastrophe. Greeks still use the word *Katastrofís* to describe the Greco-Turkish war of 1922, the destruction of Smyrna, and the exodus of the Greeks from Asia Minor. These million and a half refugees were the ones who, following the treaty of Lausanne, returned destitute to a motherland that no longer wanted them; brought back with them the music and customs of other places; and gathered in suburban neighborhoods, changing the social fabric of 1920s Athens (then dubbed the "Paris of the Eastern Mediterranean" by the young Greek state, which wanted to westernize Greek culture). Thus *rebetiko* is urban music meant for enclosed spaces, to foster introspection—unlike *dimotikì*, the mother of all Greek folk music, which is meant to be played outdoors during grand celebrations. But while *dimotikì* belongs to the people of the geographic region each song represents, *rebetiko* belongs to everyone. It is boundless. It is music for exiles ev-erywhere. It has spread throughout the country, heedless of location, of social standing and of the cultural orientation of those who practice it. Born of division, it unites.

People say that during the brutal civil war, combatants would sus-pend hostilities and join in whenever someone started singing "*Ximeoni ke vradiazi*"—a great song by Giannis Papaioannou. This song broke the remarkable record of selling more discs than there were gramophones in all of Greece. Some even bought copies just to hang as art, next to photos of loved ones.

But *Rebetes* don't like to mingle or serve as anyone else's mouthpiece. *Rebetiko* is a lamentation that demands to be sung together but danced alone. It belongs to everyone, but speaks to the individual. Its sonority comes from the Orient, from Café Aman and Byzantine chant, which—to set itself apart from the Roman Church and its polyphony and harmonic complexity—mastered the art of monophony so well that it created its own unique styles of rhythmic variation and expressive force. It has absorbed many other elements as well, elevating itself to an ethnic pastiche that is more comforting than the notion of purity advanced by government nationalists.

This music still thrives today. Its devotees draw strength from the verses of its songs, which are widely known and shared. It is a soundtrack to the trials of a nation.

When the Greek national soccer team won the 2004 European Championship, members of every Greek community, from Europe to Australia, gathered in bars and haunts to celebrate by dancing the *rebetiko*, high on happiness and excitement. People tossed napkins into the air by the thousands—a custom that has long since replaced that of shattering plates on the ground. But since then, many traditions, such as Greece's Santé cigarettes, have gone the way of its shattered plates. Greece has lost its fireflies, as Pasolini once said of a similar period in 1960s Italy. It fell into debt, got hooked on low-interest consumption, and suffered withdrawal when economic realities shifted.

Rebetiko, too, is associated with drug culture. Hundreds of songs are dedicated to hash and hookahs. There are *tragudis* that contemplate the Great Beyond and its disenchanted atheism, and where *Rebetes* beg Charon to bring hash to their friends who've ended up on the other side of the river Styx.

Charon: he who ferries through Hades.

"Charon went out to collect the people . . ."

Charon, ever-present in *rebetiko* songs, represents suffering incarnate. He is the personification of death. We translate the Ancient Greek name as Charon, but we mean Charos, death in person.

You meet him the way you might meet someone on the street. You call him by name. You sleep next to him. Just as in that story by Kazantzakis: weary from its journey, death goes to rest beside Odysseus, and, drifting off alongside him, as it sleeps it has a nightmare: it dreams of life. A society's authenticity can be measured by how it confronts death. Before Charos we're all equal, we're naked . . . *ton Charo* . . . *vghike o Charos Panaghia* . . .

Charos ferries souls because he lives at a border crossing, the one between existence and nonexistence.

Rebetiko, as Manolis Papos once said, also means to pick a side. This side of the river. That side of the neighborhood.

There again is *kríno*, from which derives the word "crisis." To choose. To sort. Rebetiko music always tunes into crises because it forces us to choose. To clearly differentiate between who we like, who we want to hang out with, and who matters little to us. To clearly choose what we're made of.

I sought out Papos myself one day. Every night, he plays in a show called "*Amán amín*," but on Fridays, around two o'clock, he joins the rest of his group on stage at the Klimatariá Tavern. The musicians traditionally sit in chairs, like in the great film by Costas Ferris, *Rembetiko* (1983), where musicians sit still and play as the story of the town unfurls.

At Klimatarià, too, musicians sit in a row, arranged before the tavern's dining tables. They play the same instruments they always have. Guitar, bouzouki and the baglamas.

On the occasion of my visit, the soccer player Dimitris Papadopoulos drank retsina and poured forth his experience of the past three years.

"The middle class is disappearing. The poor were living like shit before, too, and now it's worse than ever. But it's the middle class that's falling behind to the point of extinction. In Greece, 85% of the population owns their own home. It's how we do things, our mentality: we work our whole lives, and own our own homes, and don't waste money on renting. It's the same in Italy. Now, all the new taxes are property taxes. They tacked on a property tax and combined it with the electric bills. If you don't pay the tax, they cut off your electricity. That's illegal. Electricity, like water, is a public commodity—you can't take it away just because I didn't pay my property tax. But that's what they did. And then they took the money from that tax and put it in a Swiss bank. This is forcing people to sell their homes and rent for the rest of their lives."

"But what can we do?" I asked.

Dimitris laughed derisively. Sitting at his usual table at the Klimatarià, he began to speak with animation in his beautiful Greek-inflected Italian.

As he spoke, the musicians played a *Tsifteteli*, an oriental rhythm. Two women rose and started to dance in front of the orchestra. This is the kind of music that inspires belly dancing. Its lyrics usually evoke exotic dreams, like the *mangas*: dreams of living like a lord, or pasha. Women. Smoking. Carpets. Dreams of the Orient. Spices. The Harem—this is how the *Rebetes* had their fun. *Tsifteteli*! But then, suddenly, a *Zeibekiko* started up, and things took a turn for the worse. "This road led me back to your house and your shuttered window. In the space between us, I feel more keenly the weight of its lock. I stand before it, in front of your garden, shedding tears . . ."

"And what's this part about?" I asked.

"Horse race betting. I'm owning up to having lost money. I'm performing a *mirolòi*, a funeral pyre, the lament for the money I lost at the races."

The Ancient Greeks believed that in order to mourn, one must become one with the corpse, which is why they lay in the dust, in the quiet that surrounded the dead. Dimitris was doing it for the money he lost— he lay down beside it and sang.

That's part of the old school of thinking, from the wrong side of the tracks. Then came the Kolonaki school of thought, from the eponymous upscale neighborhood, and gave rise to the *archondorebetiko*, the aristocratic *rebetiko*. This is what we see in nightclubs and lounges, along with the four-course *Bouzouki* popularized by Manolis Chiotis, which has had a westernizing influence on *rebetiko*. And then came Keti Dali, the godmother of *skiladiko*. *Skiladiko*, or music of the dogs. A *Skilú* is a woman who sings *skiladiko*, and Keti Dali was the first and most authentic of these. When she did it, in the sixties, it was pretty. What came after that wasn't pretty, it was the butchering of Greek music.

Bouzoukia venues, where *skiladiko* is performed, were once like a stage. Going to a show was like going to a place where everyone was equal. It was like in soccer: the ball doesn't care who you are. Everyone merged together. Conventions were lost and all became equal. Songs entered our souls and made us all feel the same things whether we were rich or poor, in the same way that sickness and death treat everyone equally. It was like a drug flowing through you, apathetic to its vessel. *Bouzoukia. Skiladiko*. The stage. The tavern. Environments that shattered differences and social statuses. It was like a Carnival (*carnem levare*

56

means to remove the flesh, even in Greek), a celebration of the world inverted.

Maybe it's called *Skiladiko* because it draws out our inner animal. First, it's the whisky, then the music, and then we start to toss flowers or plates into the air, one after the other. We place no limits on ourselves. We bark and that same animal emerges, impelling us to sing at the top of our lungs, all together, songs with obscene lyrics. All anyone has to do to understand is look at the stage at six in the morning. It's like the barbarians have arrived.

Confronting death is like performing a *skiladiko*, or being on stage. We don't have a choice anymore, we can no longer hide behind that grand life accomplishment we always thought we'd achieve. Our instincts take over . . . people are no longer divided between the great and small. If the earth is above us, all of humanity rises with it. If the earth is below, all of humanity falls.

Rebetiko, too, has a tradition of shattering plates, but only as a way to vent pain. Its songs permeate our bodies and conquer them so that they no longer belong to us, but to pain. And pain can cause us to lose control of our actions. It is life that touches death.

Some believe the name *bouzouki* comes from the Turkish word *bozuk*, which means "mistake," because harmonizing it often caused the music to go off-key. *Bozuk*: the Mistake. Maybe because it's an instrument that's prone to error.

A whole song on waiting for a letter to come by mail: "I Await a Letter." Then, a love song: "My Love Will Heal You."

"If a woman said that to you, wouldn't you go crazy? Aren't we all just waiting for the day when someone will say that to us?" sighed Dimitris wistfully.

Then, another *Tsifteteli*. Two women rose from their tables and began to unravel harmoniously into oriental movements.

"Two men could never dance like that, they'd lose their identity."

The two women moved their bodies with abandon, struggling to keep themselves from spilling out of their silk blouses and tight skirts. They weren't young.

"Look at them. Some might say they're ugly. Yet, look how beautiful they are," said Dimitris, pouring himself a drink.

"There's no such thing as an ugly woman, only men who don't drink."

"What do the lyrics say?"

"It says: 'What do you care if I drink? What do you care if I smoke? What do you care if I'm the biggest whore in Babylon?' "

The music weighed in once more: "What did I do to you, my dear, to make you go away and leave me here alone? Who can be more important than me? Do you want to drive me crazy? You're throwing me away like garbage. You'll be sorry one day. You'll come crawling back. You don't care about me . . ."

The music suddenly stopped. This is how it goes with these songs. The music breaks off and the story ends. Just when we were starting to get used to it, it's over. Without frills. Definitively. Just like in life. No great speeches or long goodbyes. Just the end.

Bouzouki severs stories like a blade. This happens often with the music of pain. It is music that rises from below, like the fog of humanity, born of its sewers. Pain is a presence, carried like a ball and chain. It is both suffering and punishment, the penalty paid for living. Even when they're upbeat, songs about pain still express it, because they know how thin the line is between euphoria and death. The people who know pain have long carried melancholy in their souls. These are people who have founded civilizations, traversed oceans, taken over the world and then lost it. Italians, Greeks, Portuguese, people who were forced into nostalgia by history itself. Just as with the Jews, their destiny is to be always and everywhere unappreciated. And so, too, with the gypsies, who more than anyone else indulge their suffering, so as not to leave anything behind.

"*Rebetes*. Who were the *rebetes*? Those who dedicated their lives to this music. It was a way of life. On the fringes of industry, pop, trends. People who didn't care about getting rich.

"The Greek word for 'work' is *dulia*. Slavery. The idea of laziness as a vice has only recently come about. It once meant 'the free man's time.'

"The *rebetes* were simple people, with fewer problems. They weren't social climbers—they sought their pleasures elsewhere.

"To practice *rebetiko* today is a way of avoiding the clubbing scene, the social mechanisms that lie behind it, and the commercials about the latest trends. It's to stay at home, in one's element, with music that speaks to you, and not to someone you don't even know.

"Music can be a form of identity. But be careful: there are those who seek identity through music, and those who seek it through history. That's when the trouble begins. Nationalism for example. Against immigration, against the Germans. And the far-right is rising. Dangerously.

58

Nationalism. Ethnic purity. *Megali Idea*. We know it well. The Turks weren't the only butchers in history.

"*Rebetiko* came from forced change. Smyrna was once a prosperous and beautiful city, but its wealthy citizens ended up destitute in the suburbs of Athens. Our national hero, Kolokotronis, apparently couldn't even speak Greek, because he was Romanian. Greece is the biggest police state in the West. The one with the least amount of sovereignty. Ever since the first loan arrived from England, after our independence in 1821, we've been blackmailed. Ours was the first European country to resist this. But then came the Civil War, and outsiders have been pulling the strings ever since.

"But this is the first time that Greece, which has always been ten, twenty years behind, has found itself ahead of the others. It's an experiment. The Italians are a people that tolerates. You tolerated Fascism, Berlusconi. Greeks are less tolerant. They're more rebellious, more insurrectionist. There's a thread that unites us, even if the overused expression, "*una fatsa, una ratsa*" ("one face, one race"), isn't exactly true. But Greek debt isn't all that important—percentage-wise, we're a small country. Ten million people. Proportionally, it can't be that big of a problem. The fact is that we're lab rats in an experiment to see how banks take power. How they can take people's savings directly from the banks. We're one step ahead, but from ahead, you can look back. So look at us. Look ahead. Can the same mechanism not also apply to you? To everyone else?"

And with that, the conversation died down. The musicians sitting in chairs, arranged in a line like a platoon, sang the last song, one by Tsitsanis.

Composers are cited in *rebetiko* performances as Old Testament prophets are cited in church. Each composer's style is recognizable, just like in classical music. They belong to the myth of Creation. *Rebetiko* lives on because it is still performed. Its songs persevere because they belong to everyone, though new ones are no longer written. Maybe too much has changed. Men have changed. Maybe the next *rebetiko* will be written by an Albanian, a Pakistani, a newly arrived immigrant. *Rebetiko* is there for the taking, and its composers are legion. The golden age. And so it lives on, emanating from the mouths of men and instruments. It lives on while Papos, dressed in mourning and wearing an impassive expression, accompanies a singer through a song about an orphan: *Ta ksena cheria ine macheria*.

It says: "The hands of others, on my body, are like knives when they're not family. Those who promised me my life held no soul in their lungs. The touch of strangers, on my body, are like knives . . ."

She sings for everyone.

THOMAS IOANNOU

"Without My Future"

(poetry)

Translated from the Modern Greek by Christina Vallianatos

Without My Future

I come without my future
Poets that I admired
Turned their back on me
Girls that I loved
Feed statues in the squares
Desires turned to stone
That became public spectacles
At night I stay awake
Singing dissonant dreams
To the beaches where I had lain
Under the moonlight
I never returned innocent
I no longer recognize
The voice of my own faith
I am not he
For whom the rooster calls
Every dawn

IANA BOUKOVA

"The Stone Quarter"

(fiction)

Translated from the Bulgarian by Angela Rodel

How can I explain that I don't even need to dream? It's enough just to look at the wall in my room. Or simply to look around. As a rule, when I try to retell my nightmares, I use the system for retelling nightmares. I sit on one of the guests' laps and start crying silently. The guests are very impressed by silent crying. Far more so than by the loudest scream. "Oh," they say, their lips rounding like zeroes. The first thing I see on their faces is annoyance. After surprise. Annoyance at their surprise.

The women most often cover my face in kisses. Their lips become damp from my tears, their cheeks also grow wet, their makeup smears and afterwards I have to wash it off my face. That bit with the kisses is convenient, because then they aren't forced to speak. They figure that the kisses are enough. The men, however, are forced to speak. This occurs after a certain awkward silence. "As a child I had a boat," the men say, "that was named Tobias. My father always said that boats should have female names, because that brings good luck. But I named it Tobias instead. I always wanted a dog with that name." Here the story ends without a point, just as it began. I don't know why men think that such a story is enough to stop my tears. No one listens to my story.

* * *

People become revolting when they die. At least that's what the ancients say. No one knows that I can read. I haven't shown anyone that I can, either. The study is full of books with red and brown bindings. They are about the ancients. The others, with black bindings, are about laws. There is something hypnotizing about reading laws. Completely soporific. From them I learned that everything has its precisely defined punishment. The ancients are also in agreement about this.

The ancients depict the dead in a terrible way. They drink the blood of black animals. This blood is black. I've never seen black blood. Mine is red. They look like those rapacious birds with female faces that steal travelers' food, whatever they don't manage to devour, they trample and shit on. Sometimes I think the guests in this house are dead. Ancient dead men.

* * *

Very often I mix people up. I even mix people up who cannot be mixed up. For example, I often make a mistake and sit in the lap of someone whose lap I've already sat in. This becomes apparent immediately. Their leg muscles tense up. The person says in a suddenly cheerful voice: "Hello, what are you doing?" In such cases, the person immediately turns to my mother, who passes by with her perfume of a thousand stars in bloom: "Venessa," he says, "your son with the beautiful melancholy eyes." That is not true. My eyes are small and get red easily. They also very easily get crusty. Sometimes it happens that I've been with some person and afterwards, when I chance to look in the mirror, I see that the whole time I've had a crusty in my eye. And the person politely pretended not to notice it. Or he really didn't notice it. Or he really didn't notice me.

* * *

My mother passes by with her perfume of a thousand stars in bloom. There is stardust on her eyelids. My mother is more beautiful when she doesn't talk than when she talks. She's the most beautiful when she doesn't smile. When she smiles, two pairs of angular wrinkles appear on either side of her mouth. Like giant quotation marks. Otherwise her teeth are nice, white, almost translucent. My mother never has lipstick on her teeth like most women, who look like they've just been sucking on some dirty, half-scabbed-over wound.

I think that if my mother were a panther, she would lick my face every night before I went to sleep. With her pink tongue, through her sharp, clean teeth.

* * *

Evening, dusk, when the light is gray between the trees and makes objects and their shadows almost equal, from my window I see the body of the messenger in the garden. Ripples of dirt—a piece of his clothing, an overturned stone—his tossed-aside shoe, his deeply rooted hand clutching at the soil. It gradually grows dark and the picture becomes clearer. In the house the first lamps are lit. The message never arrives.

* * *

Otherwise during the day the garden looks perfectly in order. The gardener passes between the bushes. His gait is uncertain, as are most people's. Only that the gardener is old and can't disguise it. He prunes back branches, levels out the walkways, gathers up the dead birds. He grabs a bird by one wing, which opens up like a fan. Its body and the other wing, tucked next to it, almost drag along the ground. Hunched over, he reaches the fence and throws it as far away as his strength allows. On the way back he brushes his hands together as if after a job well done. One of his eyes waters the whole time. Indifferently, like a natural phenomenon.

* * *

I live in a remote place and this affects my contacts. I do everything I can to answer to my name, even when I can't recognize it, accompanied by drawling, diminutive suffixes. It is so easy to be impolite—to not turn around immediately, to not hear, to not answer. The bad thing is that whatever I do, everyone covers up for me. The shards of a broken glass disappear within seconds, spattered clothes are wiped clean or changed without commentary, the person whom I've slapped across the face with a careless gesture smiles, as if this were completely natural. I know it's not right. I've read the laws, too, perhaps not all of them, but I know what they're about. Yet despite this, whatever I do sinks beneath a pile of smiles, pats on the back, changes of subject, well-meaning laughter. I lie in my room and try to guess what the point of this conspiracy is. The curtains by the window are heavy and shiny, as if it's Christmas or something. The lampshade creates semi-darkness. The vicious rabbits from my earlier years still hang on the walls. Coupled up, they dance in meadows of trimmed grass and fake daisies. They wear short jackets with big buttons and bright colors. Have you noticed what a predatory animal the rabbit can be, what dastardliness lurks in his tiny eyes, how threatening his gesture can be, when he holds his little paws tucked beneath his belly, the half-opened mouth, his flat, sharp teeth, ready to sink into your throat? I use them in the evening to exercise my fear. So much effort. Just for one day, just in one room. Otherwise, my window is large and the view is nice.

* * *

In the evening the city burns with its millions of embers. In the morning the smoke rises, reaching all the way to here. A sacrifice I have not wished for.

* * *

I think I was mistaken in my first description of the guests. One mustn't get carried away by one's negative feelings. Perhaps we see things best when we are not present. Observing from the outside, through the half-open door. Perhaps our absence offers the only possibility for objective observation. Things become clear, take on outlines, undistorted by the direct confrontation with our gaze. And no one else's gaze can disturb our coldblooded appraisal. Now I see them from here, through the crack in the door: tall, untouchable, the muted conversations, the pink cocktails in their hands, the soft music. Time does not touch them, nothing touches them. Surely the ancients would have a good laugh over my attempts to make sense of this.

* * *

The letter A resembles a gnomon. I don't know where that thought came from. The ancients say that we never really learn anything, we merely recall that which we've forgotten. I remember the word "gnomon" every time I recall how the man with the deep dimple in his chin wrote the first letter on the sheet of paper. He was enormous. His palm practically filled up the page, while his torso blocked out the rest of the world. His voice was deep, hoarse, like those fake flowers in Nana's room where you can feel the wires beneath the velvet. Most of the time I sat there frozen, my hypnotized gaze fixed on the dimple in his chin, that third eye, meaty, blind, stuffed full of flesh . . . He never got tired of repeating the same thing over and over, day after day, for months. I would open my mouth, sounding out the syllables in my mind, trying to imagine that deep, assured voice coming from my lungs. I would gasp for breath. His patience was merciless. The voice of a man fulfilling his duty. "Venessa," he once said to my mother, with slight surprise at his own words, "we mustn't bury our heads in the sand. He must meet others of his own kind." A phrase that sliced through my stomach with something akin to pleasurable anxiety. My own kind?

* * *

When someone asks my mother a question, she tilts her head to one side, such that her left shoulder is almost pressing against her cheek. The question passes by the curve of her neck, without touching her. In half-profile, her eyelids are indolent, they weigh on her gaze, but her smile takes precise aim. And everyone is happy with her answer.

* * *

Of course, he was teaching me how to write the alphabet. His powerful hand would settle the fountain pen between his fingers with ease,

70

almost with tenderness. His letters were magnificent, far more beautiful than those in books. They resembled those winged women from paintings, who had stopped for a moment, but whose flight could still be seen in their bodies' striving. I could cry for hours, remembering his letters. He would wrap my hand around the pen, his hand around mine. Whirling around the circle of a small a, through the curves of an s or g was as full of happy dizziness as an amusement park (here I imagine an amusement park). Left alone, my helpless hand traced out the angular symbols, resembling printed letters, uneven, hideous. Even now, when I write out whole pages, trying to follow the train of my thought, my letters only resemble letters.

* * *

In the evenings my mother shuts my eyes with a kiss. Before that she performs a whole series of needless actions. She switches the places of several objects on the nightstand, smooths out the wrinkles in the curtains, tucks the covers under my body such that I look like a cocoon and can't move. She leaves the night light with its shade on for some unknown reason. Then she shuts my eyes with a kiss, first the left one, then the right. She crosses the room. Her dress rustles, her perfume leaves a glowing trail in the darkness beneath my eyelids. She stops at the door. I never can gather the courage to look at her, not even through veiled eyelids, in those few minutes before she shuts the door behind her. I never know whether my mother stands there looking at me or with her back to me, facing outward, towards the darkness in the hallway, where she has not yet turned on the lights, or whether she has stepped across the threshold and has turned her head towards my bed. Perhaps it isn't a few minutes, perhaps it is a very short time. But in it, there is something of the rabbits dancing with bared teeth.

* * *

Mornings begin with Nana. She bursts into my room with noisy gestures, turns out the lamp by my bed, pulls aside my Christmas curtains. The sun is a punch in the nose and I never manage to blink in time. She kneels down by the bed and starts getting me dressed. Her hands are small and red, as if she is constantly dipping them in cold water. Her fingers move lightning-fast. She puts on my white shirt, my creased pants, first she puts on the left shoe, then the right one in her lap and ties the laces. At times I have tried to imitate the knot Nana ties on my shoes with only two precise movements, a perfectly symmetrical bow with ends of an even length, but I don't get anywhere. The skills of others render me helpless.

Nana takes care of me. She digs into the plate and lifts the spoon towards my mouth. If the food is too hot, she blows on it before offering it to me. Somewhere inside me exists the memory of Nana first chewing the food before putting it in my mouth. But it is possible that this isn't true. In our communication there is full freedom of touch and exchange of bodily fluids. She spits on her thumb and smooths down my eyebrows. She takes a kerchief out of her pocket and wipes my nose. Sometimes she follows me into the bathroom and discusses the quality of my bowel movements. "You've got diarrhea again," she says, and the reproach in her voice makes me feel guilty. I don't want to offend Nana in any way.

After breakfast, she puts my coat on me, wraps me in my scarf and we go outside. Nana's hand holds mine firmly the whole time. My hand is encased in a fleecy glove, since it is cold outside, while her hand is bare, the skin on the back of it is cracked. She holds on to me so tightly that I can feel her bones through my glove. Sometimes we go out the front gate and walk all the way to the bend, where the road curves, heading down towards the city. We stop there and head back. Nana always walks on the outside, to protect me from cars. When a car comes—and that happens only rarely—Nana stands heroically in front of me, shielding me with her body. Her hand never lets go of me. Between her arm and her armpit I manage to glimpse part of the car that passes by almost silently, slowly due to the sharp curve, its tires scattering the fine gravel on the road.

Sometimes we don't go outside, however, but stay in the garden. There Nana sits on a bench, while I swing on the swing made for me, but not very high, because Nana gets scared. The only time she doesn't get scared is when my toes are braced on the ground and I push off ever so lightly with them, rocking the swing, without ever taking them off the ground even for an instant. Then she is calm and talks to the gardener about some girl named Soledad. About the night before her wedding, when her envious sister Maria put crushed glass in the sweets to kill the groom Antonio. But things got mixed up and the sweets were instead eaten by Gabriel—a distant friend and a young man with an almost unnoticeable presence, who died of internal bleeding with a single name on his lips: Soledad. The wedding, of course, was postponed due to mourning and, the more time that passed, the more Soledad came to realize that she had actually loved Gabriel and Gabriel alone, or rather, with the passing of time, Soledad fell more and more in love with the deceased Gabriel. She took advantage of the massive earthquake, which destroyed the house and trapped Maria, who had by that time gone mad, beneath the ruins, to disappear and hide in a monastery. There Soledad washed the floors with her tears, wiped away the dust with her hair and slept on the bare ground, so as to be closer to her departed beloved. But then the civil war started and Soledad was forced to leave the monastery, without having found peace . . .

Sometimes, however, the gardener has work to do and Nana sits by herself on the bench, tears a leaf off the tree and starts picking at the soft parts between its slender veins with her little red fingers. In the end only the skeleton of the leaf is left, which strongly resembles the circulatory system in our bodies. It's not a bad idea for a person to open an encyclopedia now and again. That's how I learned that our bodies are covered with a network of red and blue blood vessels. And also that our faces are sinister beneath the skin—bloody, vicious, sinewy, with bared teeth. And deeper, beneath the muscular system, we have death, just as it is drawn in engravings.

* * *

Nana clutches her lower back and complains to the gardener. It is difficult for me to get used to the idea that I am one of them. But this explains a lot of things. The guests' condescending attitude, that constant, humiliating magnanimity. The gardener complains about the pigeons. Nasty birds, he says. Not birds, but rats, rats with wings. They eat all kinds of nastiness, reproduce, spread diseases, make a mess. And they never get tired of coming. They never learn. No matter how much I put in their food, they still keep coming back. They even peck at the corpses of their own kind (again, one's own kind!). You get sick of tossing them out, but they never get sick of coming . . .

I watch them gesticulating. This inexhaustible passion of theirs for every little trifle. Such engagement in every minuscule detail. It's not a question of age. There is something quivering in their movements, something that has been nipped in the bud. Even the newspaper boy or, say, the new servant girl with the cow-like eyes. As if even now they carry the outlines of their future wrinkles, the traces of defeats yet to come. Broken. Mortal.

The gardener takes us to his tool shed to show Nana something. "You only need a few drops," he notes proudly. There is some kind of X on the label and a squashed zero, which in all likelihood is supposed to be a skull and crossbones. The gardener definitely lacks any artistic abilities whatsoever. I expect some more striking color, but the liquid is completely clear. Nana, who is always bored by someone else's topics of conversation, begins complaining about her back again.

* * *

My afternoons are free. Nana takes a nap. It's then that I go to the study. The air is stuffy and most times it is cold, because there is no reason to turn on the heat there. It turns out I am pretty hardy when it comes to cold. Someone, not very often, dusts in there and whoever it is clearly doesn't notice that some books have been moved. Most often I sit in the big armchair under the reading lamp. There is a plaid blanket that I can wrap myself in. The smell of stubbed-out cigarettes comes from somewhere close by. I am sure that if I were to search through the cupboards, I would find an ashtray full of cigarette butts that no one has thought to empty. That way I'll know what brand of cigarettes my father smoked. But that strikes me as completely useless information.

There are no pictures of him, not on the desk or on any of the walls. "Poor child," Nana says sometimes, passing by the door of the study. "Poor child." She just loves that phrase. The furniture is older than in the rest of the house. Perhaps my father adored some time different from the present.

The ancients say that at some point the world can repeat itself exactly. But this happens exceptionally rarely. And before that happens, thousands of semi-repetitions, merely hinted-at variants, vague resemblances are possible in the endless series of likely worlds. I think that sometimes it's possible for us to try to replicate some bygone world with our own efforts. Maybe that's what my father was getting at with his old furniture.

Sometimes I come here in the evening, too. There is very little risk of anyone coming into this room. Like once, for example, when the tall gentleman with the beard led the cow-like servant girl here and bent her over the desk. A whole bunch of creaking ensued. I think I know what that is about. The ancients speak in hints about that phenomenon, but have extremely exhaustive illustrations.

I am trying to gradually order all the information I have in my head, but it is getting harder and harder. Harder even than falling asleep with the light on.

* * *

The gentleman with the beard and my teacher had a fight. Their voices echoed through the whole house. It was a titanic argument. From time to time someone pounded the table with his fist and you could hear all the glasses tinkling. Then something fell and shattered, there were muffled screams and the noise of furniture being overturned. Then somebody called the police and they took my teacher away. On the steps in front of the house, the gentleman with the beard gave instructions to the police, who listened to him with a striking level of respect. I had forgotten how huge my teacher was. More than a head taller than they were. He could hardly scrunch down so as to fit in the squad car. Everything ended with the gentleman with the beard giving the stair-railing one last smash with his fist.

Even though they had argued about fashion—it is indeed astonishing what differences in taste can lead to at times: brown shirts, red kerchiefs—I think that all of that was just a pretext. I think that I was the reason. Because he was teaching me. Because I am the son of a mortal father.

* * *

I have never seen anything more hopeless than the way Nana sleeps. It happens every afternoon. Her arms are flat along her sides, her mouth is open, her cheeks sink in with every inhalation. From her mouth comes something that is both like creaking and like gurgling, as if within Nana's innards some sort of tectonic shifts are constantly taking place. Sometimes she starts falling, letting out thin, choppy screams and searching for something to grab on to. Once I gave her my hand. I'll never forget how Nana shrieked as she woke up. It was two weeks before she forgave me. She surely sleeps like that at night, too, but it's different when it happens in daylight.

When she wakes up, it's like nothing has happened. Then I have one more hour of free time. Nana listens to the story of that girl named Soledad. Sometimes I stand next to the door for a bit and hear fragments of the action. The second civil war has already started and Soledad, disguised in men's clothing, is selling weapons to both sides so as to feed her child. The man professing his love to her is surely lying. You can tell from his voice. But Soledad, too, who answers him, certainly understands this and is lying, too. I can't figure out the game between them. I have the feeling that soon something bad will happen.

The ancients recognize the effect of this type of story, which leads to the "purging of the emotions of pity and fear." I don't know exactly how it happens, though. Nana has been crying for half a year now and still hasn't reached any kind of purging. Perhaps the mechanism worked better in the time of the ancients.

* * *

Someday he'll come back with a ring on his enormous hand: a ring with a chunk of rock in it. How do I know? I just remembered this.

* * *

I think I need to limit my sources of information. To be satisfied with that which I already have. As unpleasant as it may be, a person has the right to only one explanation of things. Almost like you only have one life.

* * *

The lame gentleman has proposed to my mother. My mother told Nana that she must find a way to tell me. Nana told me. Then she told my mother, too. It's inexplicable how, when they speak in my presence, they think that I only start hearing at the moment when they turn to me personally.

Nonetheless, things are starting to fall into place. Isn't it striking that they are twelve in number? They don't always come all together, but there are twelve of them in total.

* * *

I know that the ancients are not in unanimous agreement regarding the use of this method. The majority of them, I believe, consider the empirical investigation of some problem superfluous. But I have no other way of making sure. Nor do I have the patience to observe things repeating themselves, until some unexpected event occurs that will confirm or refute my theory. Yes, I admit, albeit with certain shame—I have no patience.

76

It's not only a question of their number. But also of their function, which over time I have gradually made sense of and puzzled out: the gentleman with the beard and the thunderous voice who loves to bang his fist on the table and whom no one ever contradicts. His neurotic wife, who almost never speaks. (My mother chased off the cow-like servant girl at precisely her insistence.) That erudite old maid with the sarcastic smile and owlish glasses. The brother and sister—both blond, attractive, athletic, she loves sports, he loves the arts. The rascally wine-lover with a knack for wild dances who sometimes barges into the house with a bevy of tipsy girls with no inhibitions. One far more mature lady with a matronly bust and a pleasant smile (when I cry, she kisses me the most). Two almost emblematic figures—the colonel, the lady of the house. And, of course, the lame gentleman with his factory.

Some, I must admit, were pretty hard to figure out. One other fellow with a beard, for example, whom I recognized only when I saw him asleep behind the aquarium one night. His face looked submerged in the greenish water amidst the fish and the swaying seaweed. Or take that energetic, eternally busy young man, whom I often see in the morning running past our fence, bouncing along on his winged tennis shoes. And my mother, most of all my mother, in whose slightly simpering name it is not difficult to discover the strict Latin "Venus," my mother, who always looks like she has just swum out of the foam of events.

I think that everything said thus far exhausts the theoretical side of the question.

* * *

I'm not sure exactly when I became convinced that no other solution exists. Time passes quickly and smoothly, without colliding with some event. And neither my days nor my books tell me anything new. I was sure that at a certain point onward, things would inevitably arrive at the bottle with the X and the O. Of course, there are numerous practical details that I must consider. It must be an evening when they have all gathered, that would make the most sense. I have to put it in something that they will all taste, perhaps the ice for the cocktails. It wouldn't be bad to cut the phone lines. I really do have to take all possibilities into account. To not allow happenstance to interfere in any way.

I know it will be most difficult during that one hour while I am waiting for it to take effect. I truly can't imagine what I will do during that one hour. Reading is out of the question. I will surely pace around my room, as I have done other times. From the corner where the shiny curtain meets the wall, to the other corner formed where the opposite wall meets the wardrobe. I will traverse this diagonal again and again, sometimes face-to-face with, other times turning my back on the rabbits. A route I have never made the effort to calculate, although it is possible that in my tens of thousands of repetitions I have covered many miles. Sooner or later the time will pass and I will go downstairs.

I think the most striking thing will be the silence. Only the music will keep playing as I approach the door to the salon. Might there be some final movement, a final glass slipping from some hand and shattering on the floor? I doubt it. Only the silence and their motionless bodies.

There is also another variant, of course. I only need think of it and my heart starts beating faster. I am expecting silence, but it won't be there. While still approaching the door to the salon, I will start hearing something, but I won't believe it. Only when I open up the door a crack, will I be convinced, because I will see them: the soft music, their hushed conversations, the glasses in their hands, their careless gestures, as if nothing has happened. Perhaps I will shut the door immediately, perhaps I will stay to watch them for a while longer through the crack, without daring to cross the threshold—invulnerable, untouchable, immortal. Surely slightly ashamed of the fact that I had wanted proof. Yet most likely happy that I exist nevertheless, albeit outside of that room, but nevertheless close to them, in their presence.

I think that in either case, the ancients would be fascinated by the results.

Editors, Authors, Translators

Jane Assimakopoulos is an American-born translator from Greek and French. Her translations include work by award-winning author Thanassis Valtinos (Northwestern University Press and Yale University Press). She has edited the Greek translations of over 20 novels by the late acclaimed American author Philip Roth. She lives in Greece.

Ali Bolcakan is a PhD candidate in Comparative Literature at the University of Michigan.

Iana Boukova is Bulgarian born and bilingual (Bulgarian-Greek) poet, writer and translator. She has published in Bulgarian two books of poetry, a collection of short stories and a novel, as well as the translations of more than 15 books of modern Greek and ancient poetry (Sappho, Catullus, Pindar). She has lived in Greece since 1994 where she is a member of the platform Greek Poetry Now and of the editors board of FRMK, a biannual journal on poetry, poetics and visual arts. In 2006 the Athens publishing house Ikaros published her book of poetry *The Minimal Garden.* Poems and short stories by Iana Boukova have been translated in English, Spanish, French and several other languages.

Vinicio Capossela was born in 1965 in Hannover, Germany and grew up in Campania, Italy. He is a singer-songwriter with over fifteen albums to his credit, and the author of three books, *Non si muore tutte le matine* (2004), *In clandestinità* (co-written with Vincenzo Costantino Cinaski, 2009), and *Tefteri - Il libro dei conti in sospeso* (2013).

Yiorgos Chouliaras is a Greek poet, prose writer, essayist, and translator, who was born in Thessaloniki, Greece. He studied in New York and now lives in Athens, after having worked in Ottawa, Washington, DC, and Dublin. He is the author of multiple collections of poetry, including *Iconoclasm* (1972), *The Other Tongue* (1981), *The Treasure of the Balkans* (1988), and *Dictionary of Memories* (2013).

Cameron Cross is Assistant Professor of Iranian Studies at the University of Michigan, Ann Arbor, where he teaches Persian literature (classical and modern), Iranian cinema, and various topics in Middle Eastern studies.

Born in 1977, **Tarek Emam** is a young Egyptian writer and journalist who studied English Literature at Alexandria University. He has published three collections of short stories, a children's book, and five novels. *The Second Life of Constantine Cavafy*, which came out in 2012, tells an imaginary tale about the poet as he reads, in secret, a novel being written about him by one Alexander Singopoulos, with whom Cavafy shared an intimate friendship.

Karen Emmerich is a translator of Modern Greek prose and poetry. She has translated a collection of short stories by Ersi Sotiropoulos as well as works by Margarita Karapanou, Amanda Michalopoulou and Sophia Nikolaidou. She teaches comparative literature at Princeton.

Maryam Hooleh was born in Tehran, Iran in 1978 and now lives in Sweden. She is the author of several books of poetry, including *The Kite Will Never Fly in My Hands* (1998), *In the Alleys of Athens* (1999), *Cursed Booth* (2000), and *Contemporaneous Leprosy* and *Hell INC* (both 2004).

Thomas Ioannou was born in Arta, Greece in 1979. A graduate in Medicine at the National and Kapodistrian University of Athens, he works as a neurologist, poet, and essayist. His work has been included in literary magazines, and his first book, *Ippokratous 15*, was published in 2011. He al'so serves on the editorial team for the Greek literary magazine *Ta Poiitika*.

Mata Kastrisiou was born in Athens, Greece in 1989. She is a graduate of the Theater of Arts - Karolos Koun Drama School and of the Department of Archaeology and History of Art of the National and Kapodistrian University of Athens. She is the author of *The Six O'Clock Garbage Truck*.

A teacher and editor, **David Mason** was born and raised in Bellingham, Washington. Mason's collections of poetry include *The Buried Houses* (1991), winner of the Nicholas Roerich Poetry Prize; *The Country I Remember* (1996), winner of the Alice Fay Di Castagnola Award; *Arrivals* (2004); and the verse novel *Ludlow* (2007), awarded the Colorado Book Award for Poetry and named best book of poetry in 2007 by the *Contemporary Poetry Review* and the National Cowboy and Western Heritage Museum. His prose includes a memoir about Greece, *News from the Village: Aegean Friends* (2010), and a collection of essays, *The Poetry of Life and the Life of Poetry* (1999). Mason teaches at Colorado College. He was appointed the Colorado poet laureate in 2010.

Elettra Pauletto is a writer and translator. She holds an MFA in

Creative Writing from Columbia University, where she also studied literary translation. Her writings and translations have appeared in *Pacific Standard Magazine, Guernica Magazine, The Iowa City Press-Citizen,* and elsewhere. She is currently translating a book on the music of Michael Jackson.

Born in 1979 in Patras, Greece, **Elena Polygeni** is a poet, actress, and musician, and has published three books of poetry, *The Land of Paradoxical Things* (To Kendri, 2014), *My Sorrow is a Woman* (Poema, 2012), and *Letters on a Blackboard* (Dodoni, 2009).

Angela Rodel is a professional literary translator living and working in Bulgaria. She received a 2014 NEA translation grant for Georgi Gospodinov's novel *The Physics of Sorrow* (Open Letter 2015)—the first time a Bulgarian-language work has received such an award. Six novels in her translation have been published by US and UK publishers. Her translations have appeared in literary magazines and anthologies, including *McSweeney's, Little Star, Granta.org, Two Lines, The White Review* and *Words Without Borders.*

William Gertz Runyan is a doctoral candidate in Comparative Literature at the University of Michigan. His research examines the dynamic geocultural boundaries of Yiddish literary discourse in the twentieth century.

A Professor of Comparative Literature and Near Eastern Studies at the University of Michigan, **Anton Shammas** is a Palestinian writer and translator of Arabic, Hebrew and English. He is the author of three books of poetry, two plays, many essays in English, Hebrew and Arabic, and a novel (*Arabesques*), originally published in Hebrew and translated into nine languages.

Chaim Shoshkes was an author, economist, and journalist, born in Bialystok, Poland in 1891. He was well known for his travel writing, widely syndicated in the Yiddish world press.

Ersi Sotiropoulos has written ten works of fiction and a book of poetry. Her *Zigzag through the Bitter Orange Trees* was the first novel ever to win both the Greek national prize for literature and Greece's preeminent book critics' award. Sotiropoulos has been a fellow at institutes and universities around the world, including the University of Iowa's International Writing Program and Princeton University. She lives in Athens. Her novel *What's Left of the Night*, translated by Karen Emmerich, is now available from New Vessel Press.

Will Stroebel is a comparatist of Modern Greek and Turkish literature, focusing on book history and textual fluidity across the Greco-Turkish Mediterranean. He recently defended his dissertation at the University of Michigan and will be working as a postdoctorate fellow this year at the Seeger Center for Hellenic Studies at Princeton University. His work has been published in the *Journal of Modern Greek Studies* and *Book History*.

Holly Taylor just defended her thesis and is currently about to graduate from Oregon State University with an M.F.A in fiction writing. Though she mostly writes about her childhood and country upbringing in rural Michigan, she has also written extensively about Greece (specifically, about her time traveling in northern Greece).

Christina Vallianatos is proud alumna of the Modern Greek Program at the University of Michigan, receiving a BS in Neuroscience and Modern Greek Studies in 2010. She is currently pursuing a PhD in Human Genetics from the University of Michigan, where she studies how certain genes influence brain development and disorders such as autism.

Peter Vorissis is a PhD candidate in Comparative Literature at the University of Michigan. He also has a Master's degree in Literary Translation from NYU and his translations from the French have appeared in *The Guardian* and *The Brooklyn Rail*.